The Easter Bunny's Helpers

Anne Mangan

Illustrated by Tamsin Ainslie

Angus&Robertson
An imprint of HarperCollins*Children's Books*

Angus&Robertson

An imprint of HarperCollins*Children'sBooks*, Australia

First published in Australia in 2013
by HarperCollins*Publishers* Australia Pty Limited
ABN 36 009 913 517
harpercollins.com.au

HarperCollins*Publishers*

Level 13, 201 Elizabeth Street, Sydney NSW 2000, Australia
Unit D1, 63 Apollo Drive, Rosedale, Auckland 0632, New Zealand
A 53, Sector 57, Noida, UP, India
77–85 Fulham Palace Road, London, W6 8JB, United Kingdom
2 Bloor Street East, 20th floor, Toronto, Ontario M4W 1A8, Canada
195 Broadway, New York NY 10007, USA

National Library of Australia Cataloguing-in-Publication entry:

Mangan, Anne.
    Easter bunny's helpers / Anne Mangan; Tamsin Ainslee, illustrator.
    978 0 7322 9576 9 (hbk.)
    For primary school age.
    Animals--Australia--Juvenile fiction.
    Easter--Juvenile fiction.
    Easter eggs--Juvenile fiction.
    Other Authors/Contributors:
    Ainslee, Tamsin.
A823.3

The illustrations in this book were created in pencil, gouache and collage on Arches paper.
Cover design and internal design by Matt Stanton, HarperCollins Design Studio
Typeset in ITC Usherwood Book
Colour reproduction by Graphic Print Group, Adelaide, South Australia
Printed by RR Donnelley in China, on 128gsm Matt Art

8 7   18 19

For Vince and Michelina, thank you so much for all your love and support. AM

For my mother Lyn, and the magical memories of Easter as a child,
full of delightful surprises and lots of fun. TA

The animals heard the news and grinned from ear to ear.
The Easter Bunny needed help with Easter plans this year.
'As well as Easter eggs, there are buns and hunts to do.
I need a special helper — who knows, it might be you!'

So Emu painted all her eggs with ochre, ash and clay. 'When the Easter Bunny sees these eggs, he'll pick me straightaway.'

Kangaroo looked in the mirror, admiring her bouncy legs.
'Bunny will see that I'm just right for delivering all the eggs.'

Koala, being cuddly, hoped that Bunny would pick her.
'I just need a hairdresser to do something with my fur.'

Cockatoo thought, with his screeching, it might seem that he's tone deaf.
'But when it comes to baking, Bunny will know I'm quite the chef.'

And just to show how keen they were, they hopped to Bunny's door,
each hoping that they'd be the one, but really not too sure.

When the Easter Bunny saw them, he couldn't pick just one.
'With so many special helpers, my work will soon be done!'

They decorated hard-boiled eggs — Emu knew what to do —
using paints, dye, crayons, stickers, stencils, glitter and glue.

Koala hid the chocolate eggs in all the secret spots —
under beds, in toy boxes and around the flower pots.

Kangaroo hopped far and wide delivering more eggs.
Bunny was so thankful for her pouch and powerful legs.

Cockatoo baked yummy buns, putting crosses on each one.
When he'd finished, Bunny said, 'It's time we had more fun —'

With eggs on spoons, they raced and rolled the eggs along the ground.

Then looked for eggs that Bunny hid and most of them were found.

As Bunny thanked them, one by one, and gave them bunny ears,
he wondered why he'd worked alone for quite so many years!